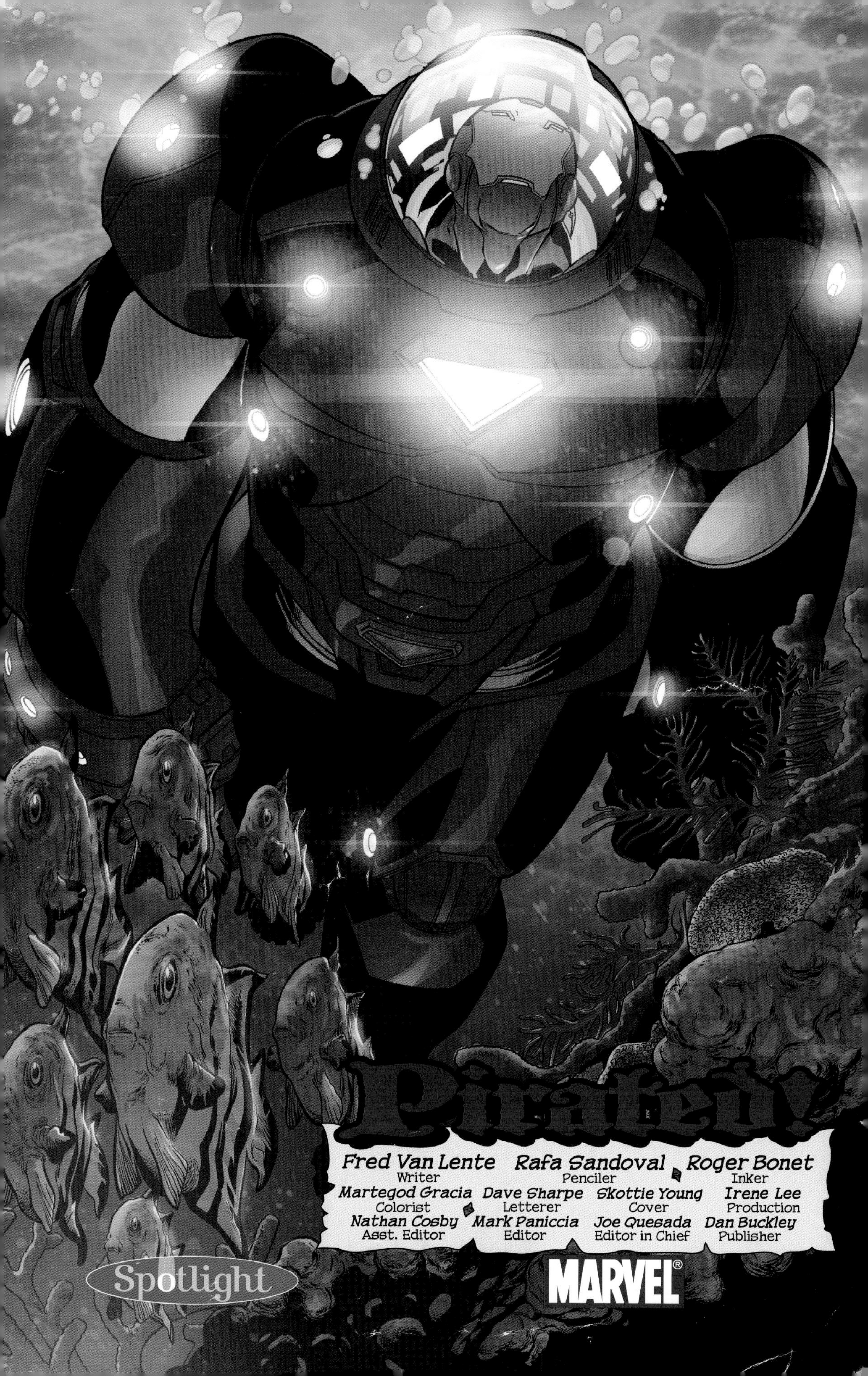

Fred Van Lente Writer
Rafa Sandoval Penciler
Roger Bonet Inker
Martegod Gracia Colorist
Dave Sharpe Letterer
Skottie Young Cover
Irene Lee Production
Nathan Cosby Asst. Editor
Mark Paniccia Editor
Joe Quesada Editor in Chief
Dan Buckley Publisher
Spotlight
MARVEL®

VISIT US AT
www.abdopublishing.com

Reinforced library bound edition published in 2009 by Spotlight, a division of the ABDO Group, 8000 West 78th Street, Edina, Minnesota 55439. Spotlight produces high-quality reinforced library bound editions for schools and libraries. Published by agreement with Marvel Characters, Inc.

Library of Congress Cataloging-in-Publication Data

Van Lente, Fred.
Pirated! / Fred Van Lente, writer ; Rafa Sandoval, penciler ; Roger Bonet, inker ; Martegod Gracia, colorist ; Dave Sharpe, letterer ; Skottie Young, cover. -- Reinforced library bound ed.
p. cm. -- (Iron Man)
"Marvel."
ISBN 978-1-59961-591-2
1. Graphic novels. [1. Graphic novels. 2. Superheroes--Fiction.] I. Sandoval, Rafa, ill. II. Title.
PZ7.7.V26Pi 2009
[Fic]--dc22

2008033397

Spotlight

All Spotlight books have reinforced library bindings and are manufactured in the United States of America.

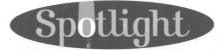

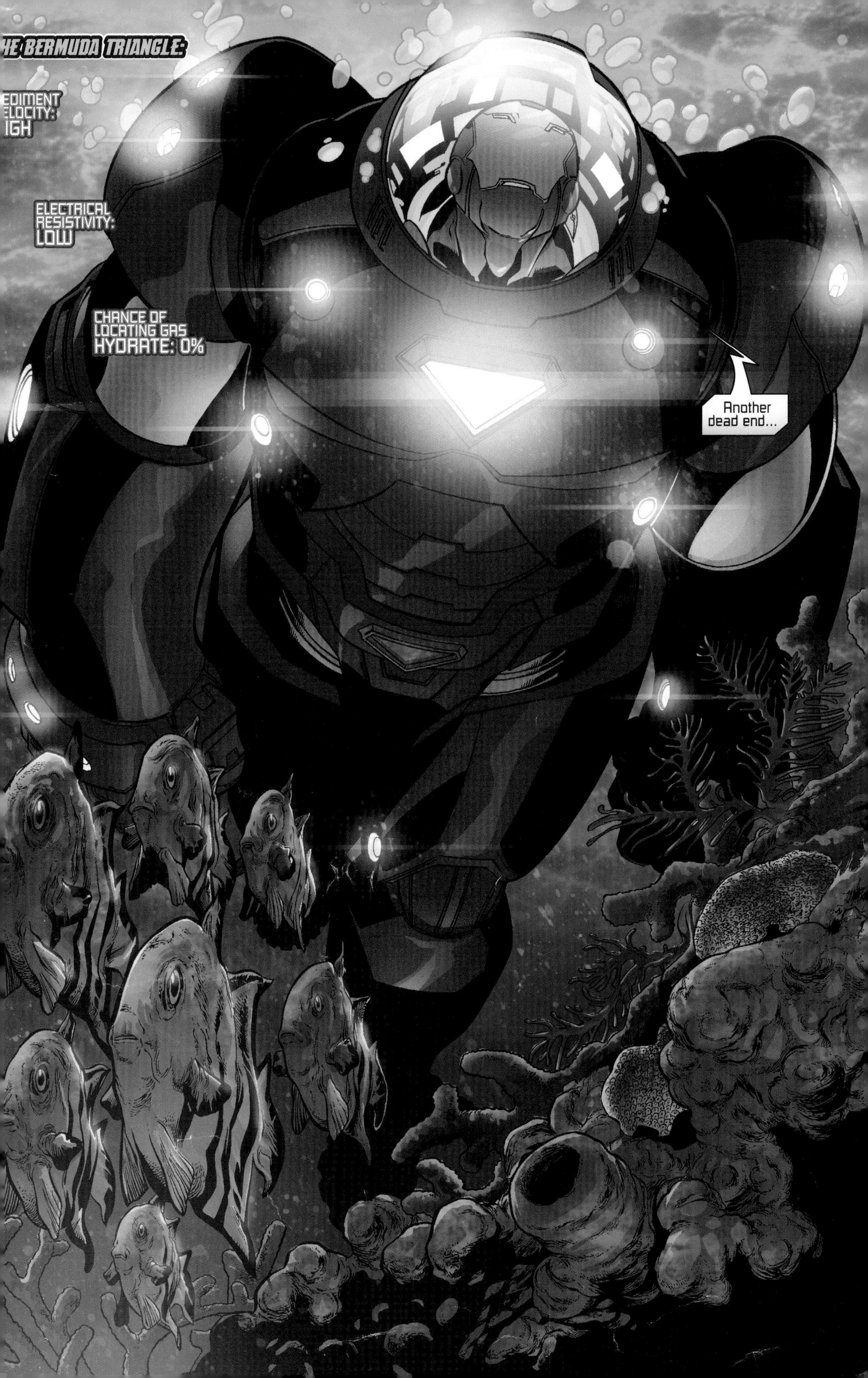
HE BERMUDA TRIANGLE:
EDIMENT
ELOCITY:
IGH
ELECTRICAL
RESISTIVITY:
LOW
CHANCE OF
LOCATING GAS
HYDRATE: 0%
Another dead end...

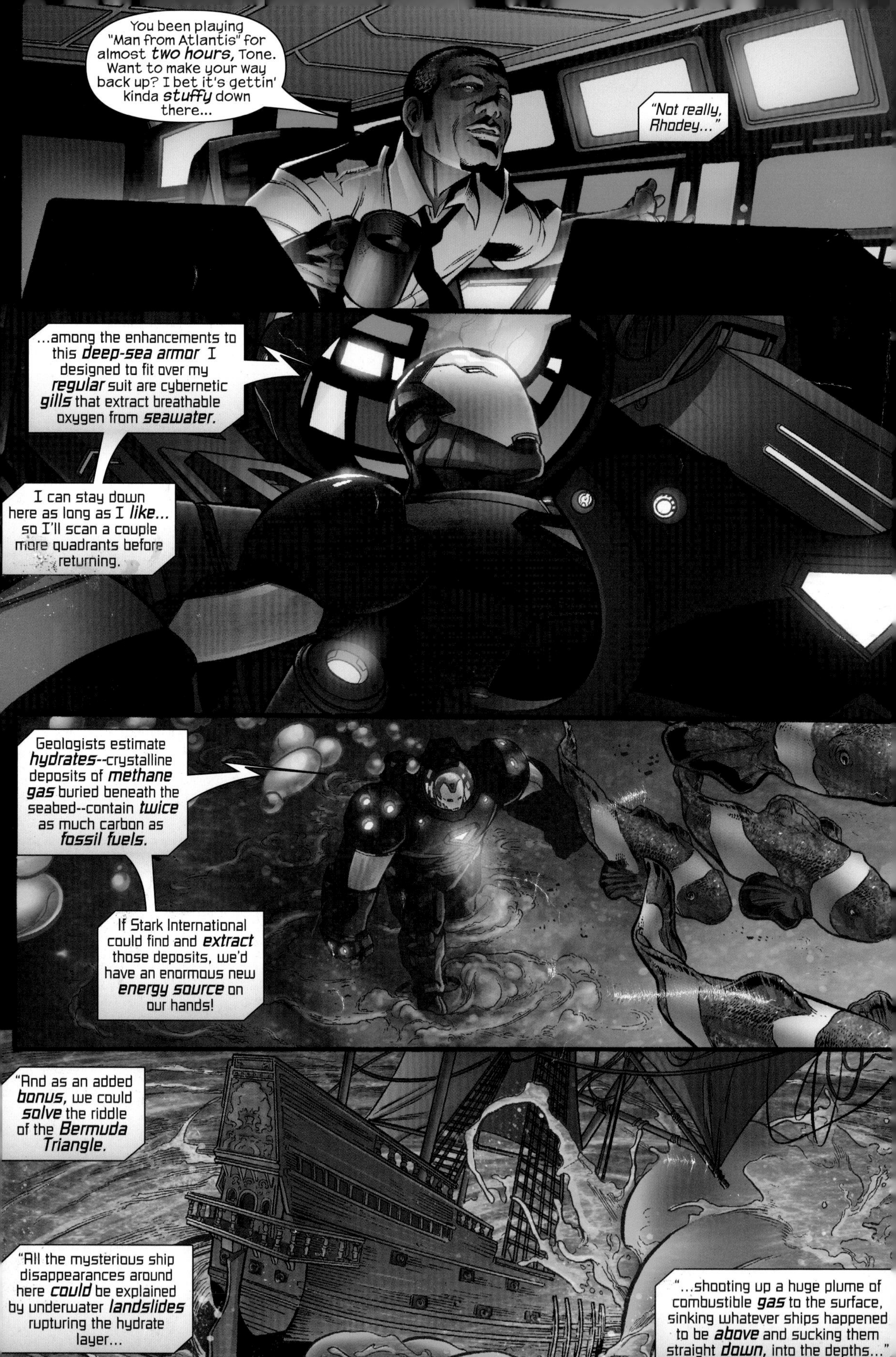

You been playing "Man from Atlantis" for almost *two hours,* Tone. Want to make your way back up? I bet it's gettin' kinda *stuffy* down there...
"Not really, Rhodey..."
...among the enhancements to this *deep-sea armor* I designed to fit over my *regular* suit are cybernetic *gills* that extract breathable oxygen from *seawater.*
I can stay down here as long as I *like...* so I'll scan a couple more quadrants before returning.
Geologists estimate *hydrates*--crystalline deposits of *methane gas* buried beneath the seabed--contain *twice* as much carbon as *fossil fuels.*
If Stark International could find and *extract* those deposits, we'd have an enormous new *energy source* on our hands!
"And as an added *bonus,* we could *solve* the riddle of the *Bermuda Triangle.*
"All the mysterious ship disappearances around here *could* be explained by underwater *landslides* rupturing the hydrate layer...
"...shooting up a huge plume of combustible *gas* to the surface, sinking whatever ships happened to be *above* and sucking them straight *down,* into the depths..."

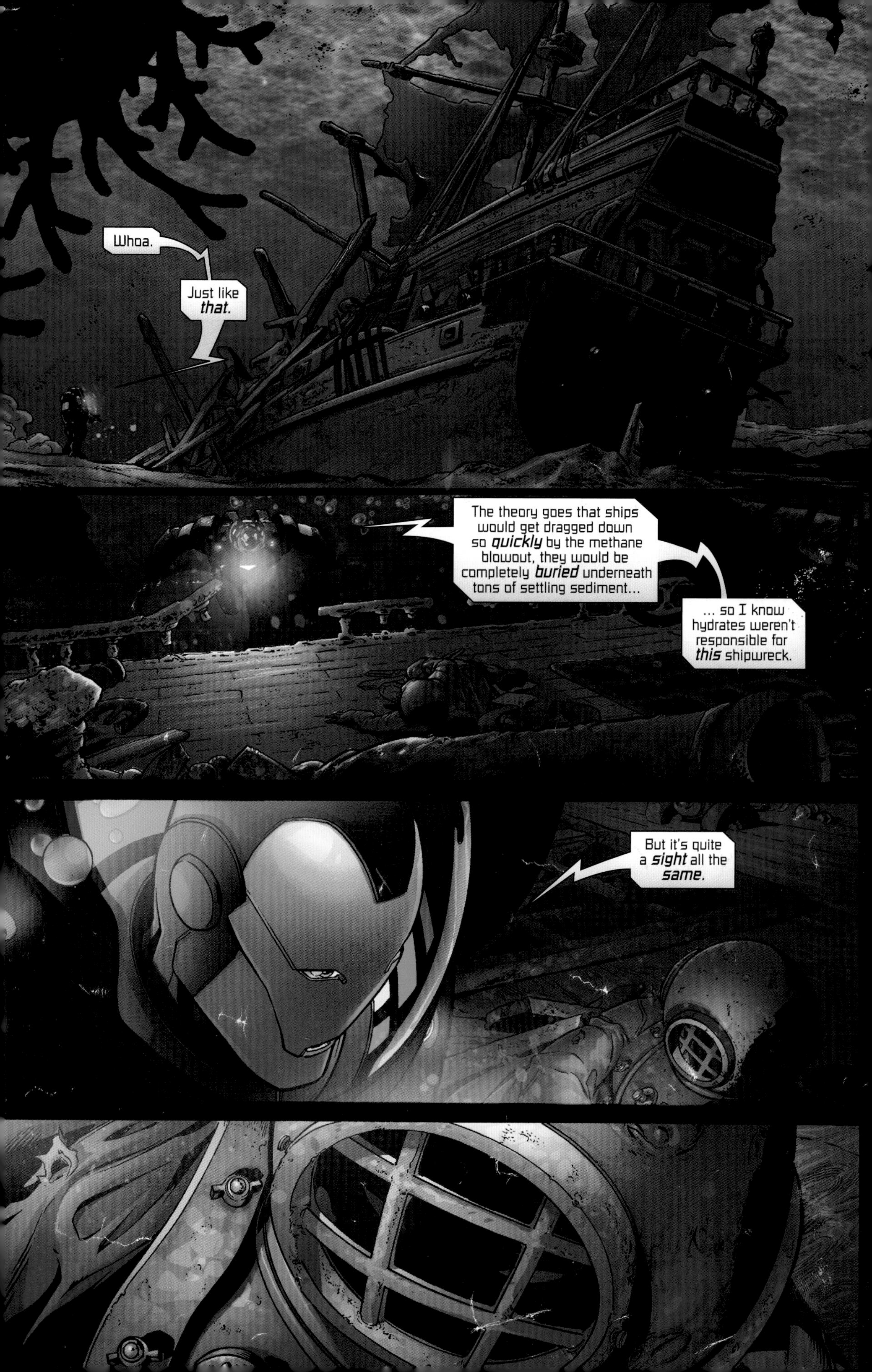
Whoa.
Just like *that*.
The theory goes that ships would get dragged down so ***quickly*** by the methane blowout, they would be completely ***buried*** underneath tons of settling sediment...
... so I know hydrates weren't responsible for ***this*** shipwreck.
But it's quite a ***sight*** all the ***same***.

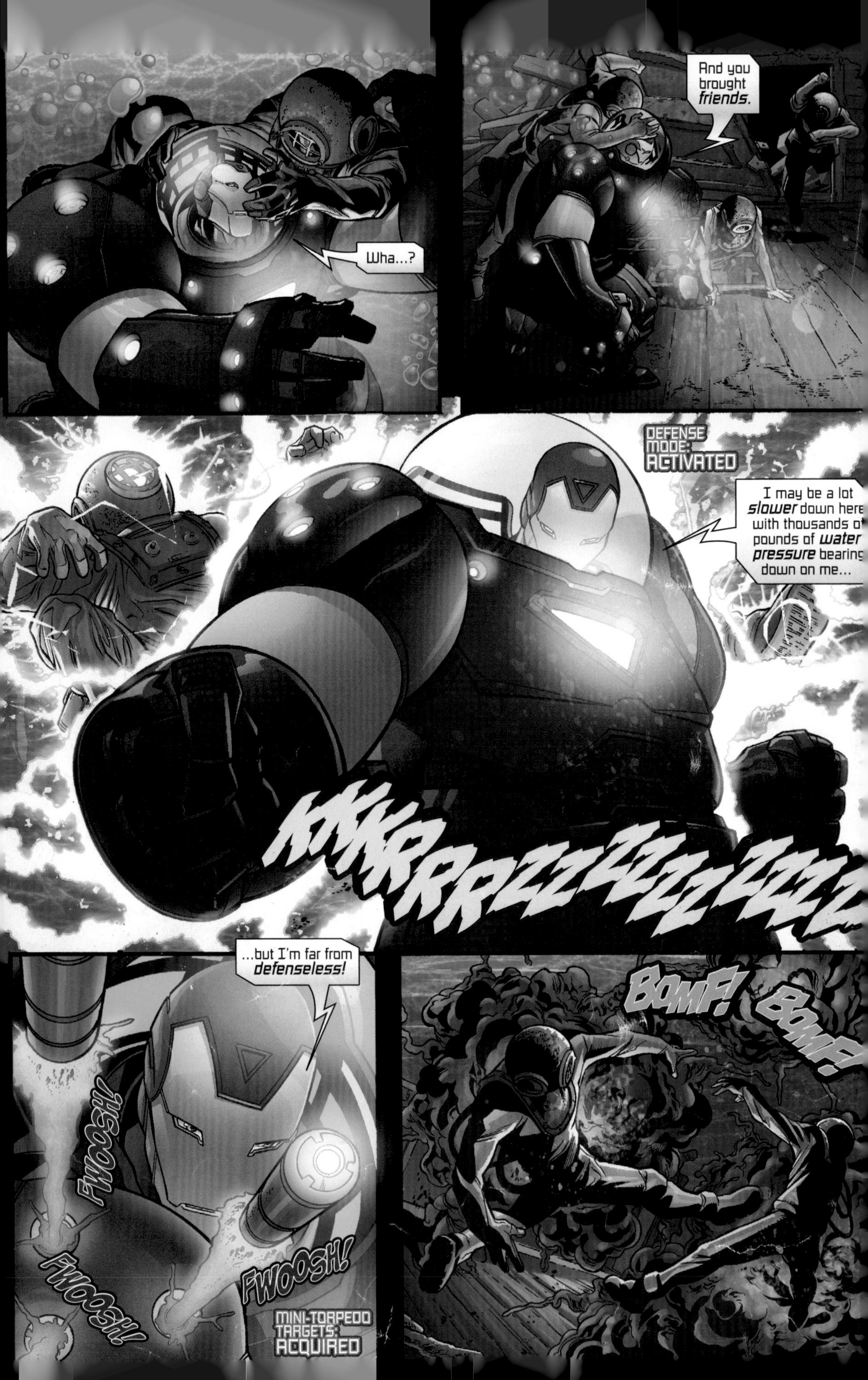
Wha...?
And you brought *friends.*
DEFENSE MODE: ACTIVATED
I may be a lot *slower* down here with thousands of pounds of *water pressure* bearing down on me...
KKKRRRZZZZZZZZZZZ
...but I'm far from *defenseless!*
FWOOSH!
FWOOSH!
FWOOSH!
MINI-TORPEDO TARGETS: ACQUIRED
BOMF! BOMF!

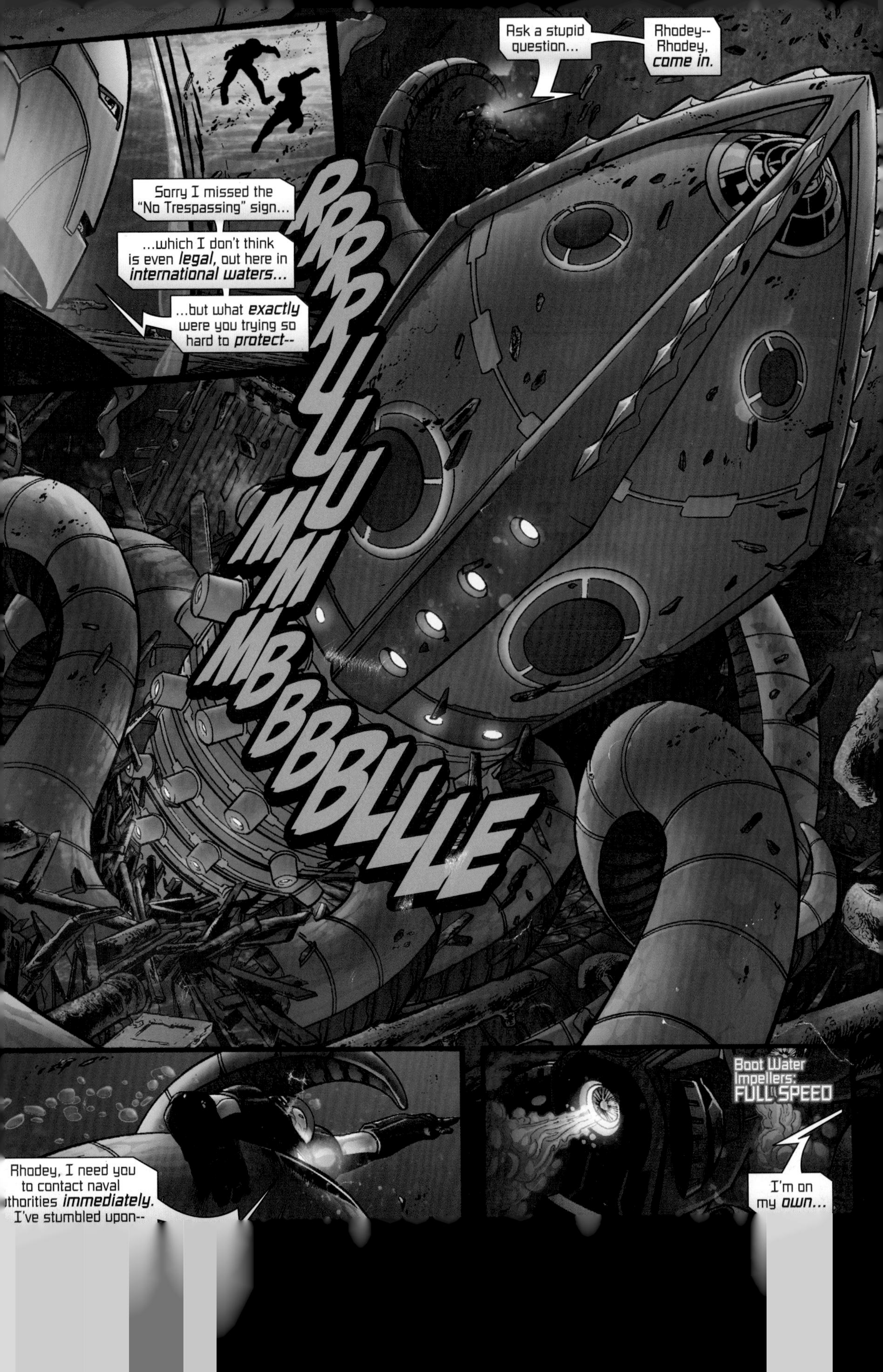
Sorry I missed the "No Trespassing" sign...
...which I don't think is even *legal*, out here in *international waters*...
...but what *exactly* were you trying so hard to *protect*--
RRRRUUUMMMBBBBLLLE
Ask a stupid question...
Rhodey-- Rhodey, *come in*.
Rhodey, I need you to contact naval thorities *immediately*. I've stumbled upon--
Boot Water Impellers: FULL SPEED
I'm on my *own*...

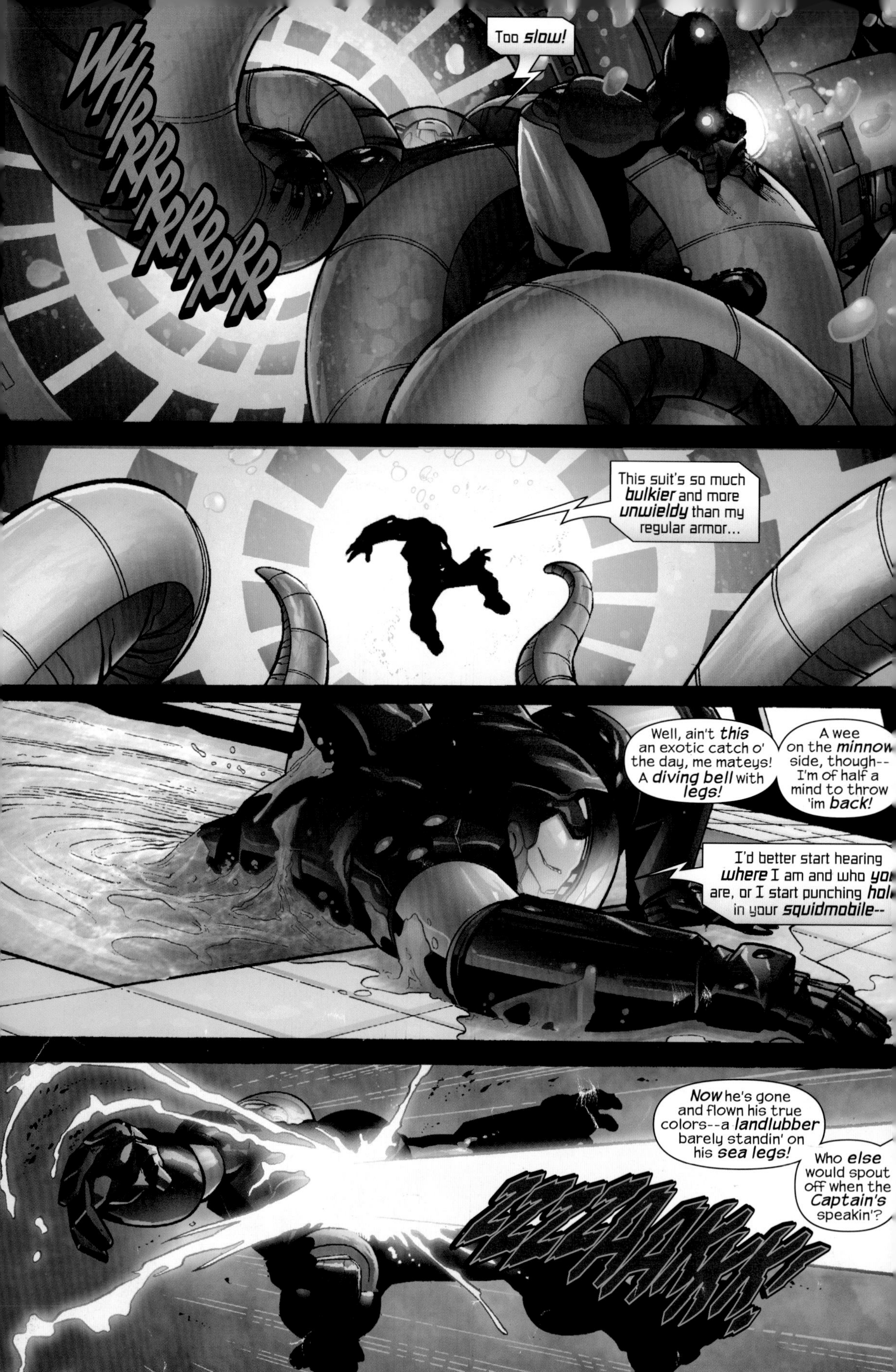
Too slow!
This suit's so much bulkier and more unwieldy than my regular armor...
Well, ain't this an exotic catch o' the day, me mateys! A diving bell with legs!
A wee on the minnow side, though-- I'm of half a mind to throw 'im back!
I'd better start hearing where I am and who yo are, or I start punching hol in your squidmobile--
Now he's gone and flown his true colors--a landlubber barely standin' on his sea legs!
Who else would spout off when the Captain's speakin'?

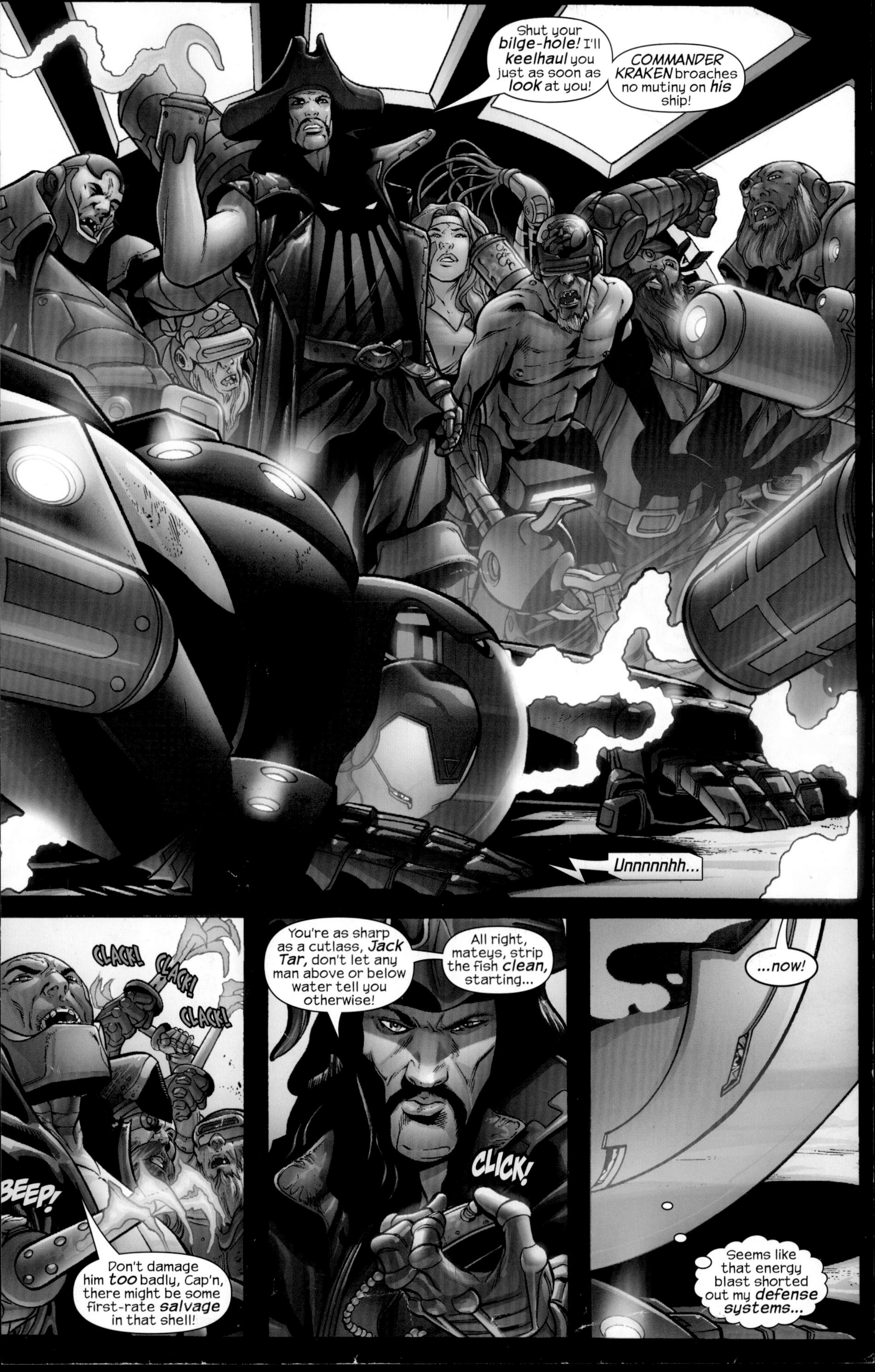
Shut your bilge-hole! I'll keelhaul you just as soon as look at you!
COMMANDER KRAKEN broaches no mutiny on his ship!
Unnnnnhh...
CLACK! CLACK! CLACK!
BEEP!
Don't damage him too badly, Cap'n, there might be some first-rate salvage in that shell!
You're as sharp as a cutlass, Jack Tar, don't let any man above or below water tell you otherwise!
All right, mateys, strip the fish clean, starting...
CLICK!
...now!
Seems like that energy blast shorted out my defense systems...

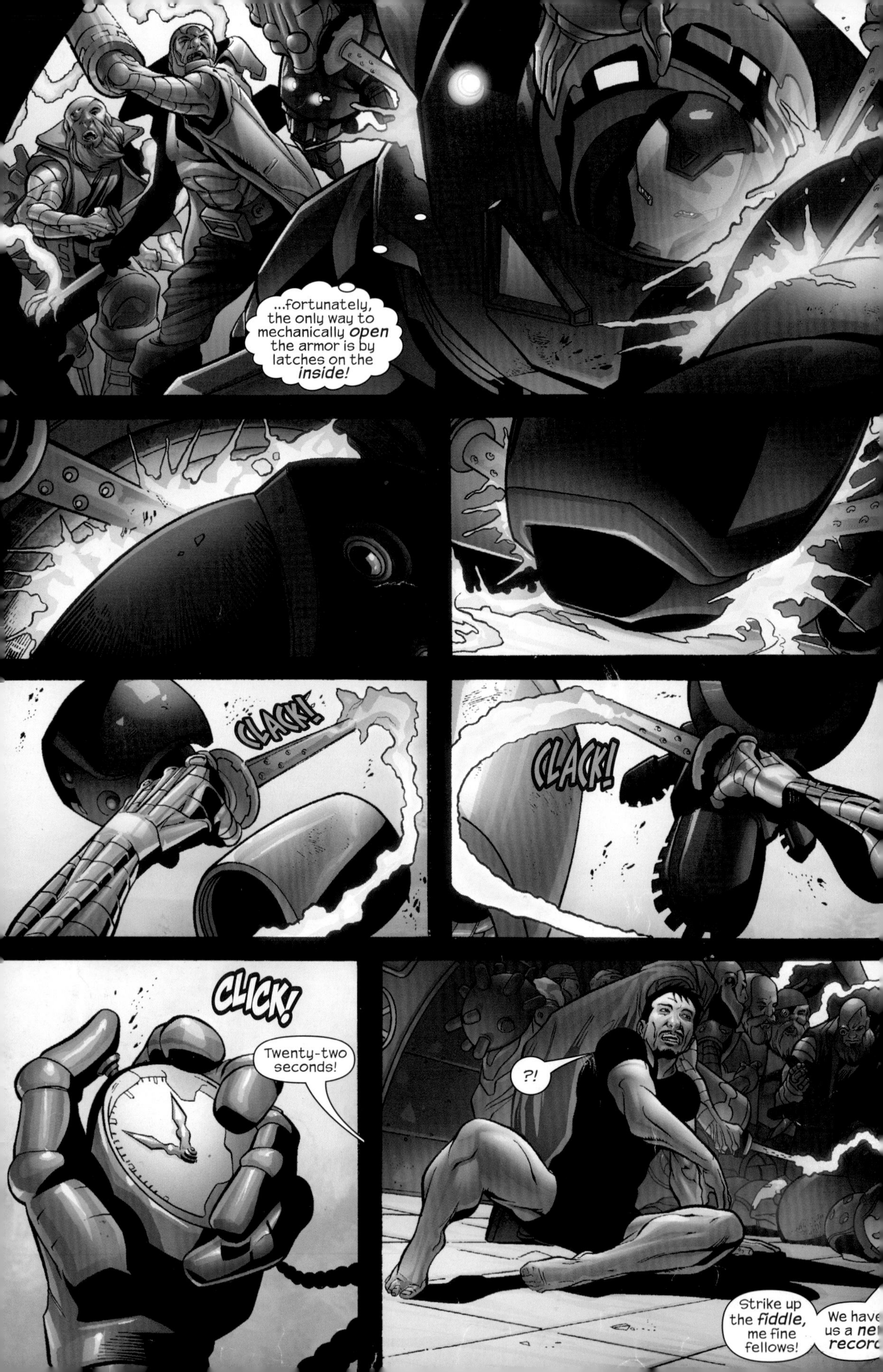
...fortunately, the only way to mechanically *open* the armor is by latches on the *inside!*
CLACK!
CLACK!
CLICK!
Twenty-two seconds!
?!
Strike up the *fiddle,* me fine fellows!

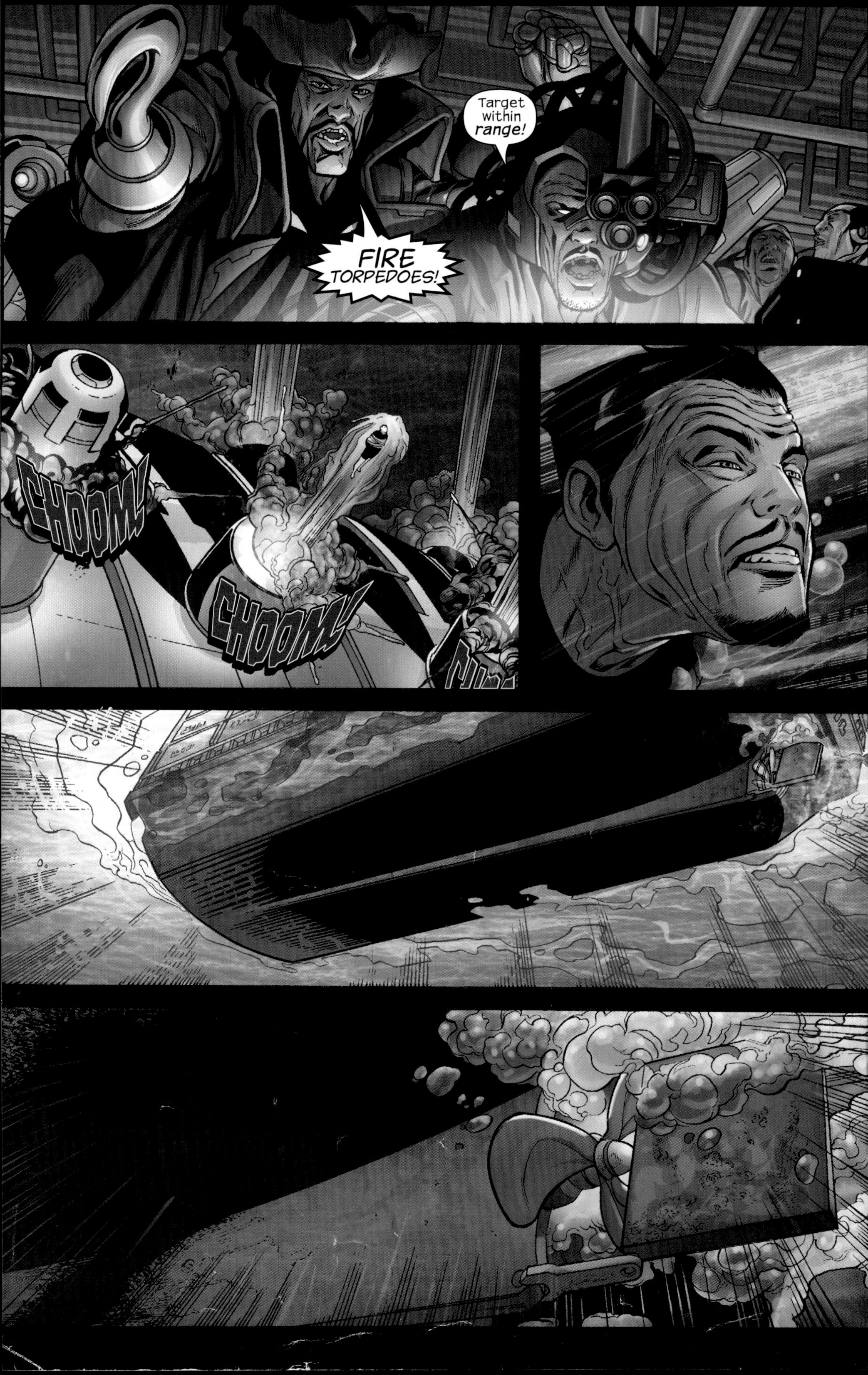
Target within range!
FIRE TORPEDOES!
CHOOM!
CHOOM!

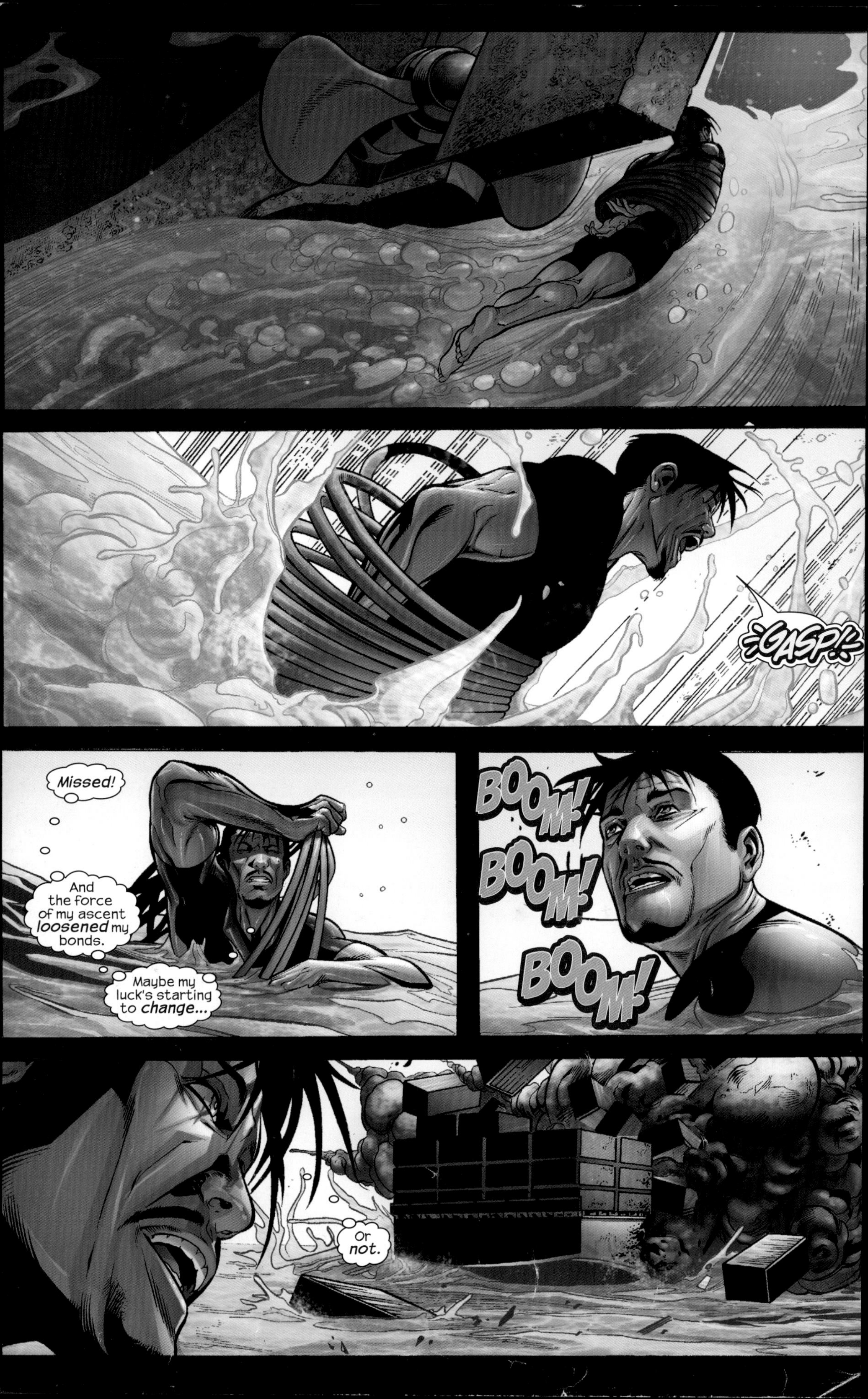
GASP!
Missed!
And the force of my ascent loosened my bonds.
Maybe my luck's starting to change...
BOOM!
BOOM!
BOOM!
Or not.

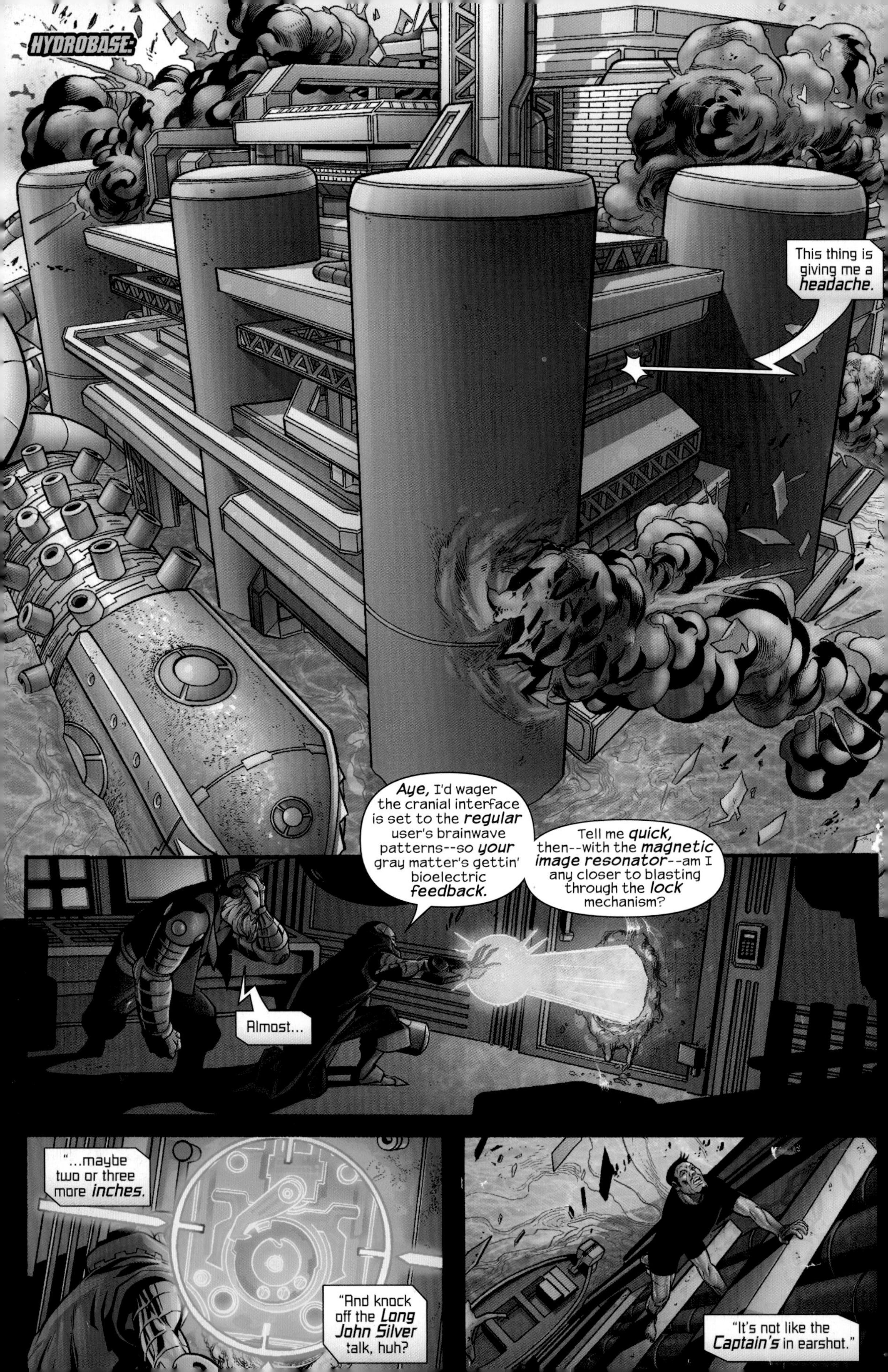
HYDROBASE:
This thing is giving me a *headache.*
Aye, I'd wager the cranial interface is set to the *regular* user's brainwave patterns--so *your* gray matter's gettin' bioelectric *feedback.*
Tell me *quick,* then--with the *magnetic image resonator*--am I any closer to blasting through the *lock* mechanism?
Almost...
"...maybe two or three more *inches.*
"And knock off the *Long John Silver* talk, huh?
"It's not like the *Captain's* in earshot."

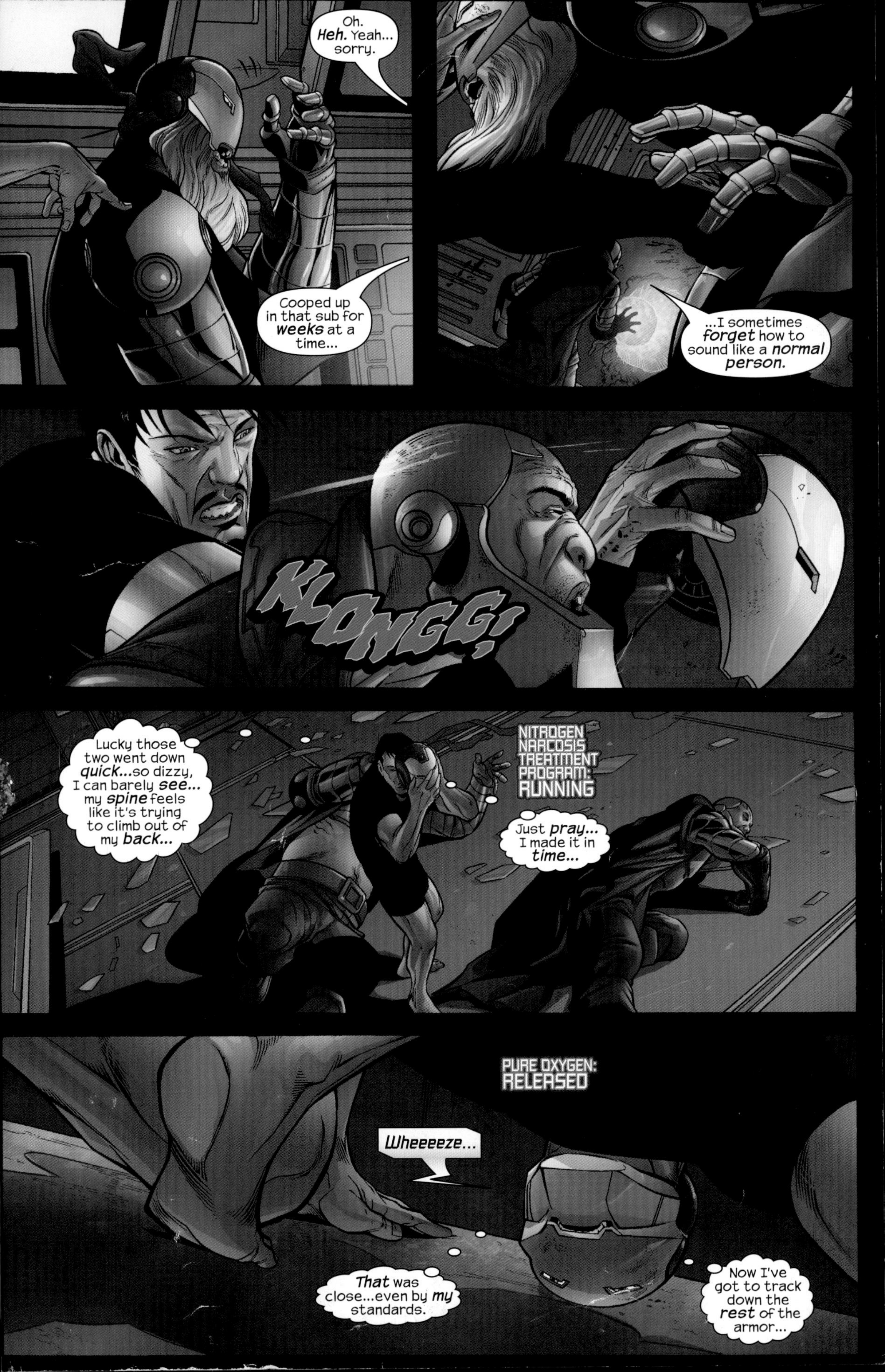
Oh. Heh. Yeah... sorry.
Cooped up in that sub for weeks at a time...
...I sometimes forget how to sound like a normal person.
KLONGG!
Lucky those two went down quick...so dizzy, I can barely see... my spine feels like it's trying to climb out of my back...
NITROGEN NARCOSIS TREATMENT PROGRAM: RUNNING
Just pray... I made it in time...
PURE OXYGEN: RELEASED
Wheeeeze...
That was close...even by my standards.
Now I've got to track down the rest of the armor...

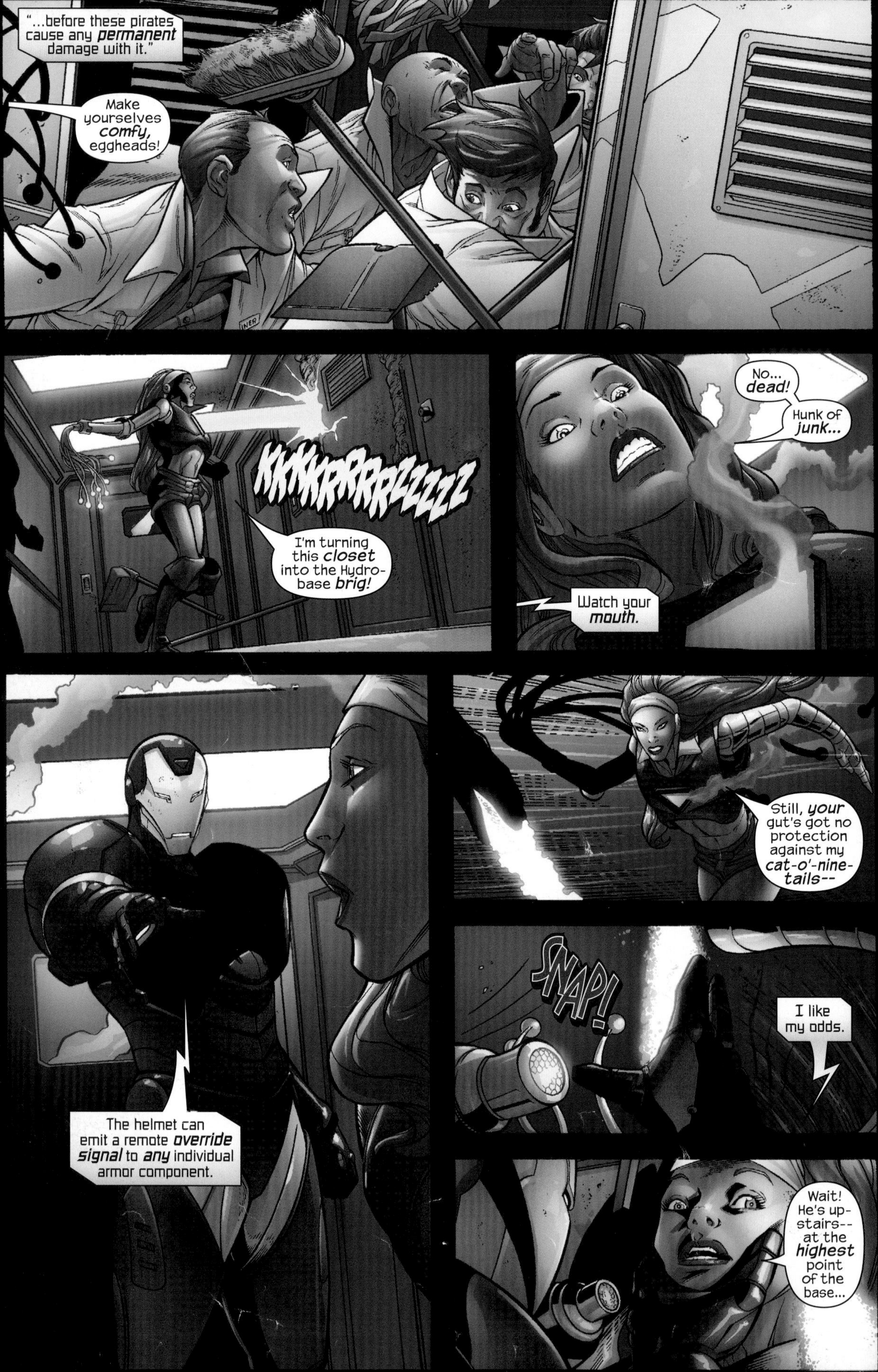
"...before these pirates cause any *permanent* damage with it."
Make yourselves *comfy,* eggheads!
KKKKRRRRRZZZZZ
I'm turning this *closet* into the Hydro-base *brig!*
No... *dead!*
Hunk of *junk...*
Watch your *mouth.*
The helmet can emit a remote *override signal* to *any* individual armor component.
Still, *your* gut's got no protection against my *cat-o'-nine-tails--*
SNAP!
I like my odds.
Wait! He's up-stairs-- at the *highest* point of the base...

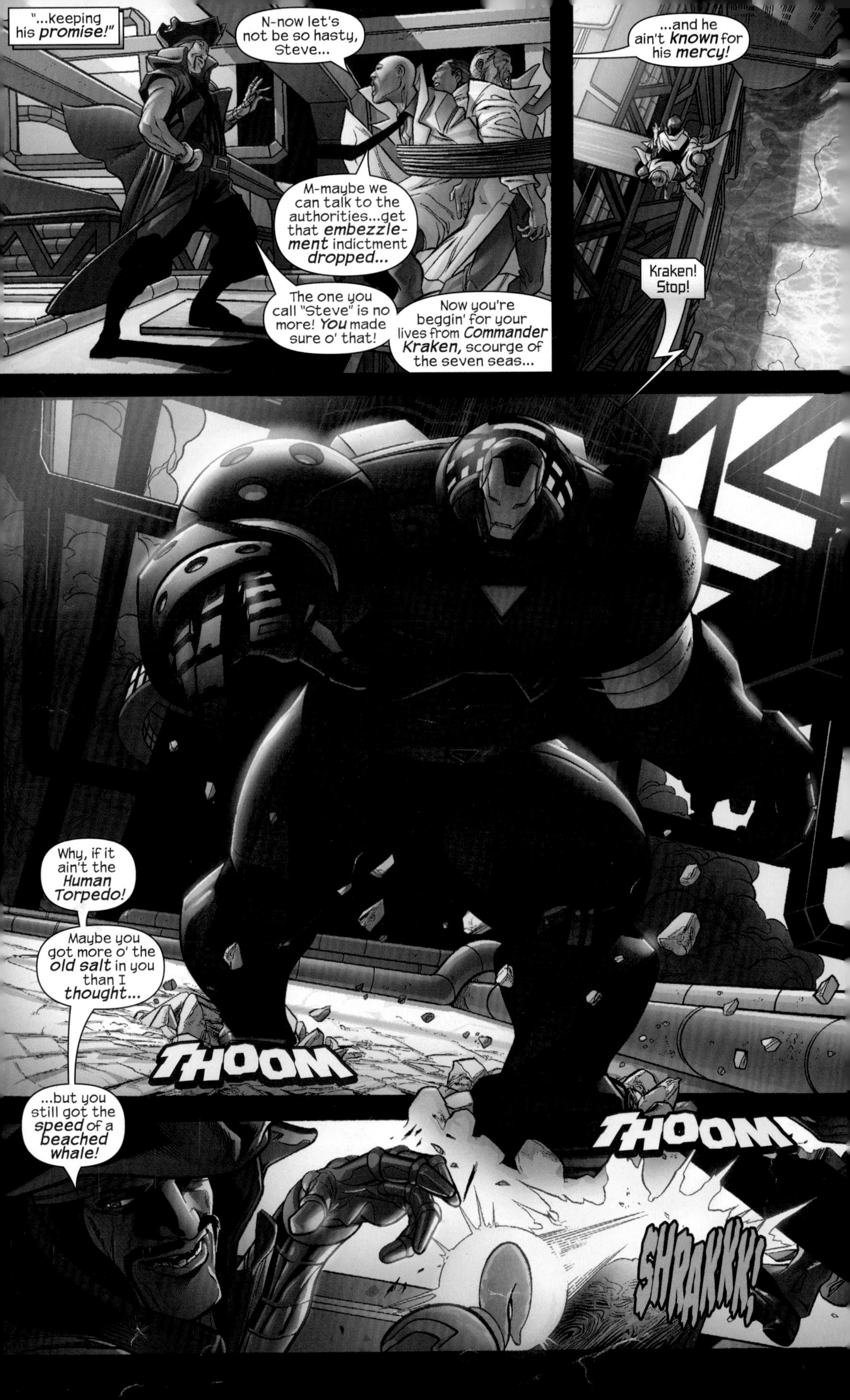
"...keeping his *promise!*"
N-now let's not be so hasty, Steve...
M-maybe we can talk to the authorities...get that *embezzlement* indictment *dropped...*
The one you call "Steve" is no more! *You* made sure o' that!
Now you're beggin' for your lives from *Commander Kraken,* scourge of the seven seas...
...and he ain't *known* for his *mercy!*
Kraken! Stop!
Why, if it ain't the *Human Torpedo!*
Maybe you got more o' the *old salt* in you than I *thought...*
THOOM
...but you still got the *speed* of a *beached whale!*
THOOM!
SHRAKKK!

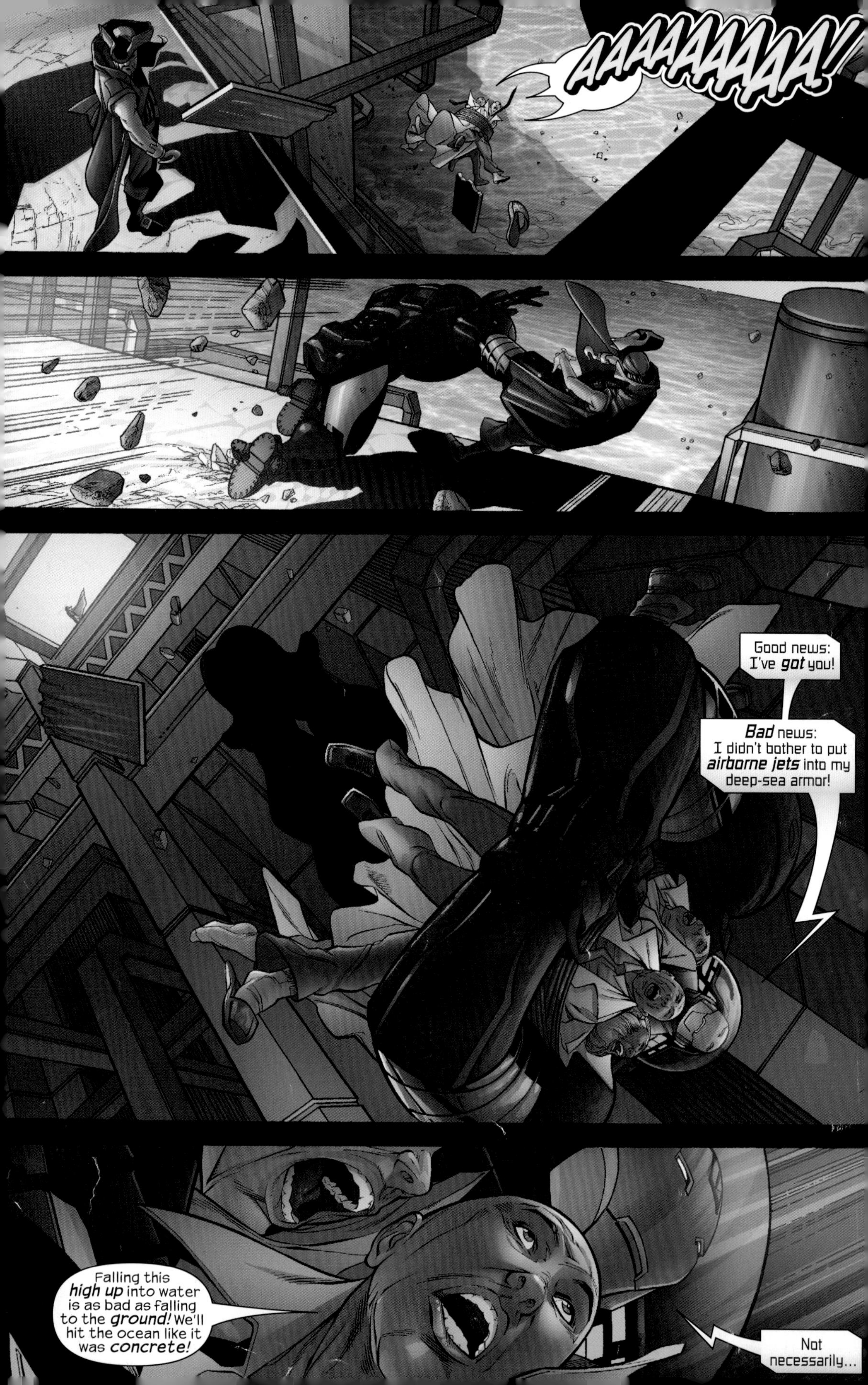
AAAAAAAAA!
Good news: I've **got** you!
Bad news: I didn't bother to put **airborne jets** into my deep-sea armor!
Falling this **high up** into water is as bad as falling to the **ground!** We'll hit the ocean like it was **concrete!**
Not necessarily...

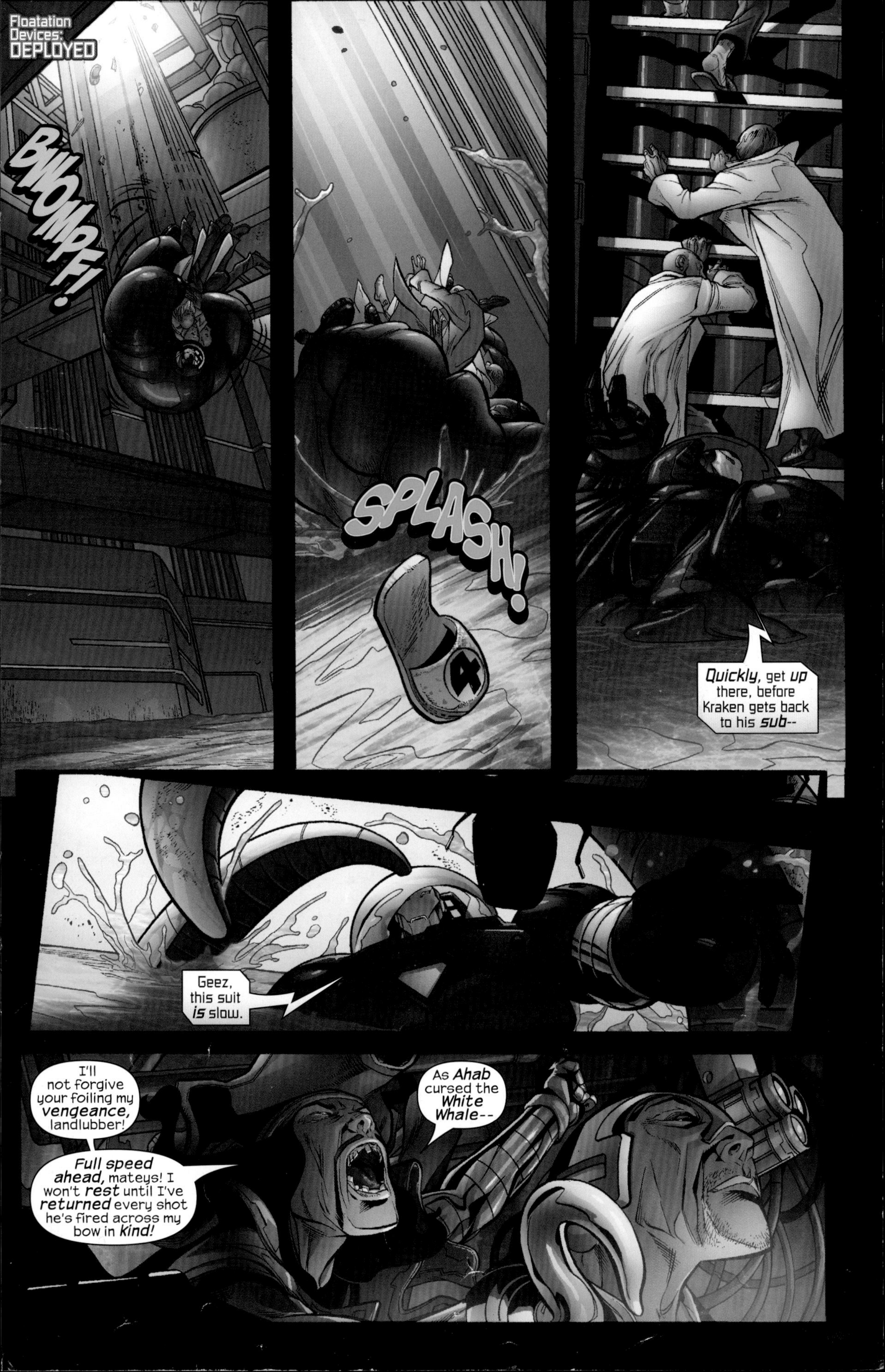

Floatation Devices: DEPLOYED
BWOMPF!
SPLASH!
Quickly, get up there, before Kraken gets back to his sub--
Geez, this suit is slow.
I'll not forgive your foiling my vengeance, landlubber!
Full speed ahead, mateys! I won't rest until I've returned every shot he's fired across my bow in kind!
As Ahab cursed the White Whale--

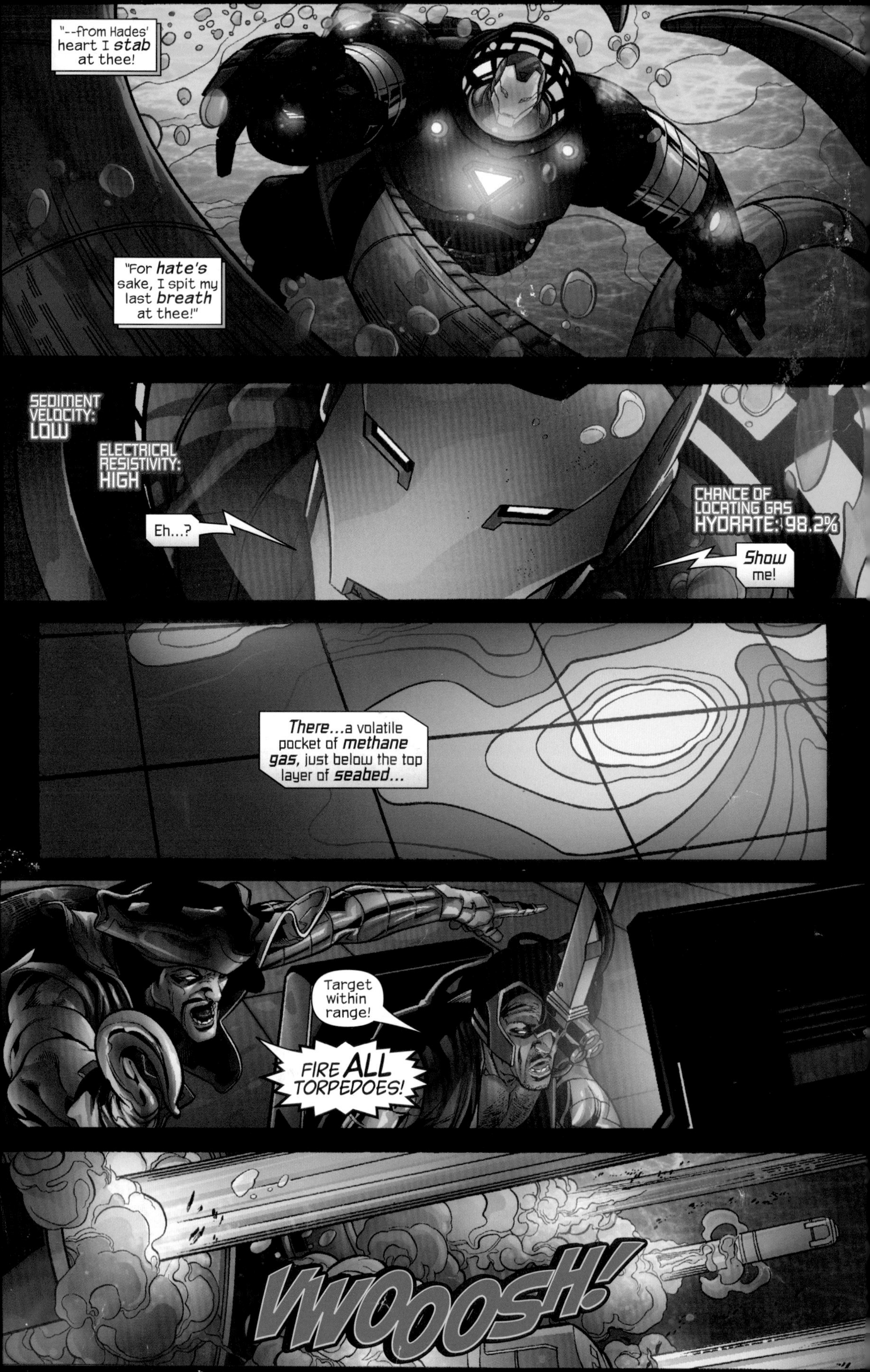
"--from Hades' heart I *stab* at thee!
"For *hate's* sake, I spit my last *breath* at thee!"
SEDIMENT VELOCITY: LOW
ELECTRICAL RESISTIVITY: HIGH
Eh...?
CHANCE OF LOCATING GAS HYDRATE: 98.2%
Show me!
There...a volatile pocket of *methane gas*, just below the top layer of *seabed*...
Target within range!
FIRE ALL TORPEDOES!
VWOOOOSH!

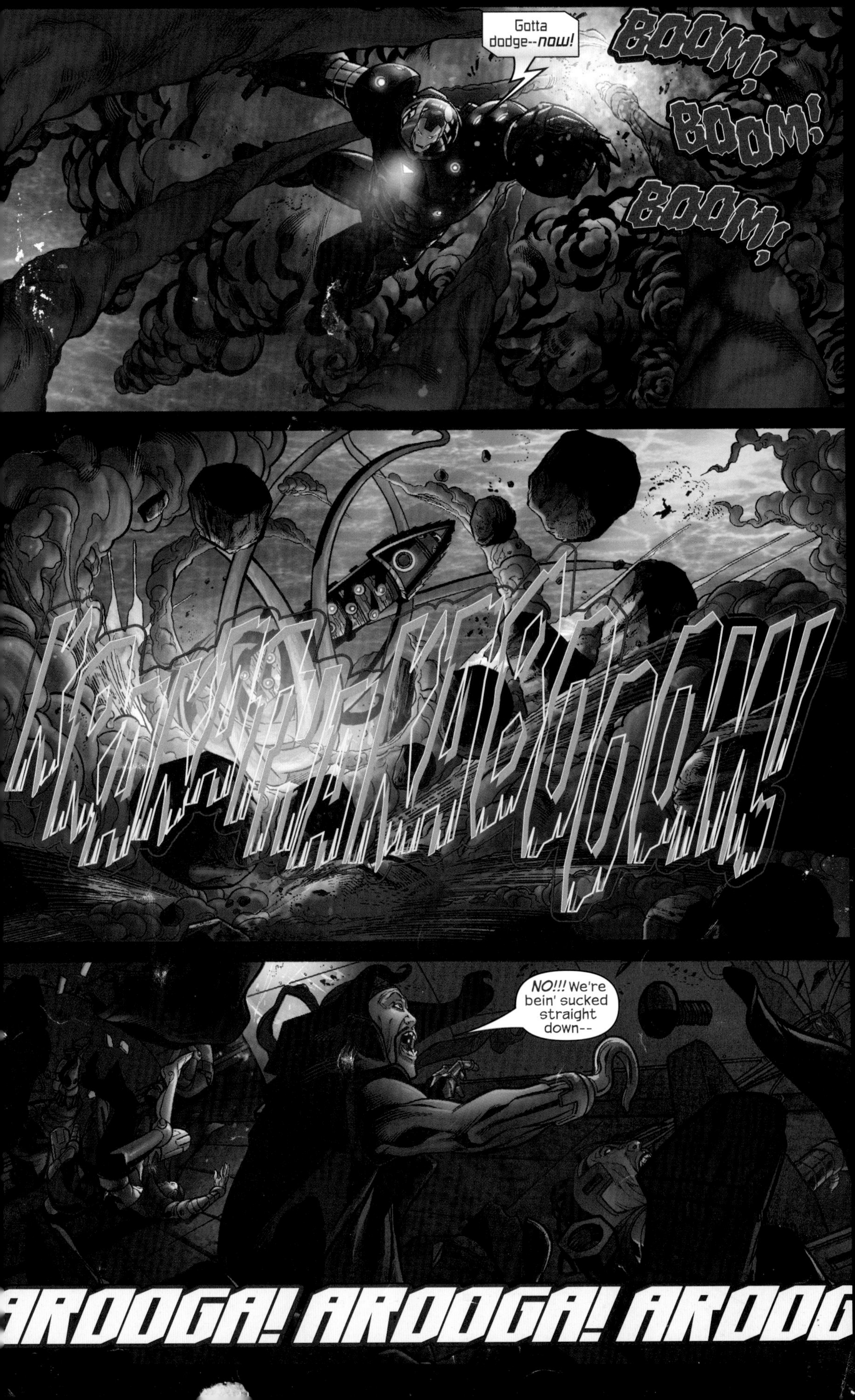
Gotta dodge--*now!*
BOOM! BOOM! BOOM!
NO!!! We're bein' sucked straight down--
AROOGA! AROOGA! AROOG

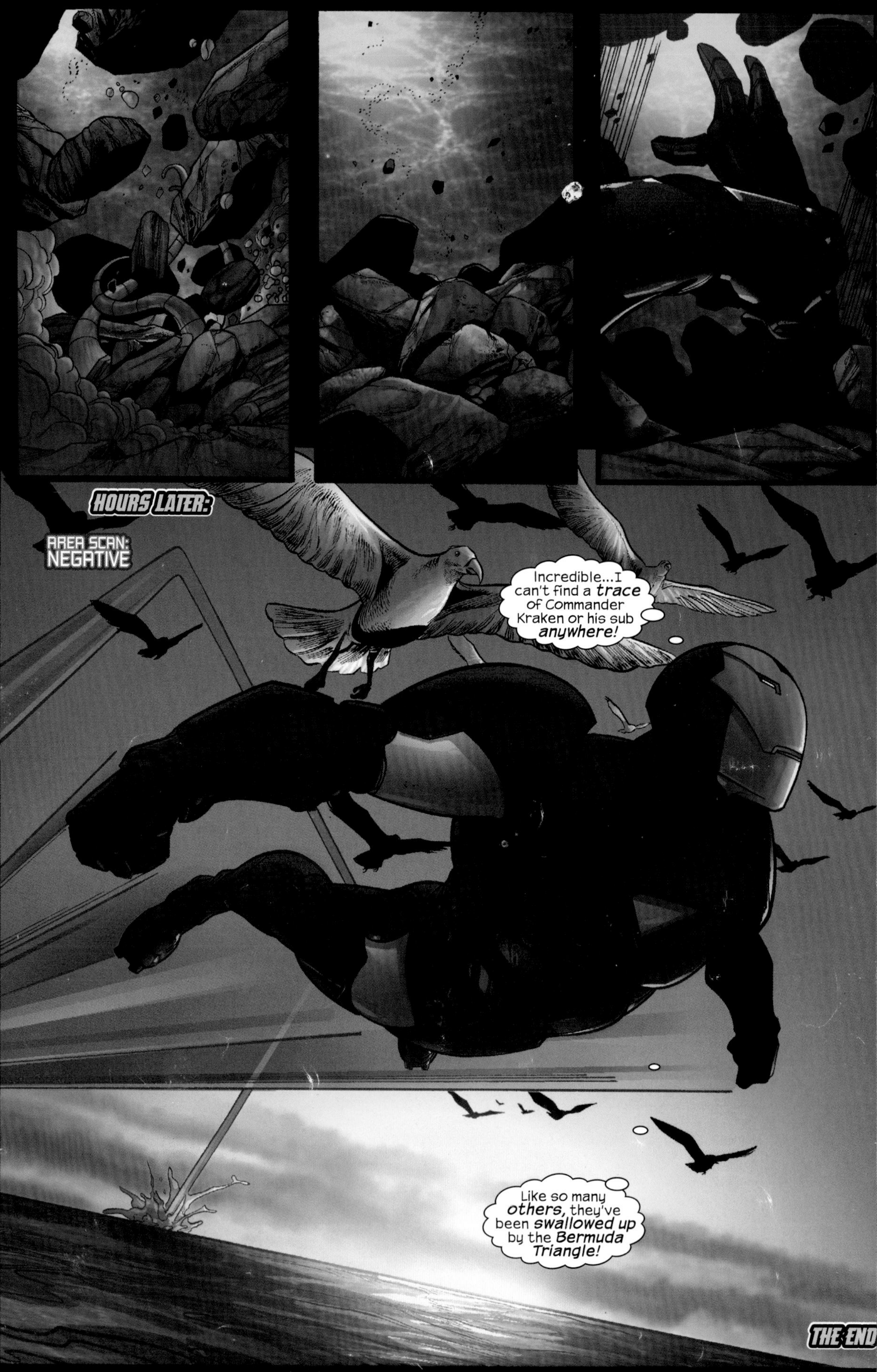
HOURS LATER:
AREA SCAN:
NEGATIVE
Incredible...I can't find a trace of Commander Kraken or his sub anywhere!
Like so many others, they've been swallowed up by the Bermuda Triangle!
THE END